For Mom
—G.P.

North, South, East, West

Text copyright © 2017 by Roberta Brown Rauch
Illustrations copyright © 2017 by Greg Pizzoli
All rights reserved. Manufactured in China.
HarperCollins Children's Books, a division of HarperCollins Publishers, 195 Broadway, New York, NY 10007.
www.harpercollinschildrens.com

ISBN 978-0-06-026278-5

The artist used Adobe Photoshop to create the digital illustrations for this book.
Typography by Rick Farley
16 17 18 19 20   SCP   10 9 8 7 6 5 4 3 2 1

First Edition

NORTH, SOUTH,

EAST, WEST

BY MARGARET WISE BROWN

PICTURES BY GREG PIZZOLI

HARPER

An Imprint of HarperCollinsPublishers

Once there was a little bird all tucked into her nest.

It was almost time for her to fly away.

Her mother taught her to ride the wind
and to fly above and below the storms,

and to glide on the strength of the wind.

And then they would fly home
to their nest in the sycamore tree
and she would sing her a song.

And the little bird would ask,
"When I fly away, which is best,
North, South, East, or West?"

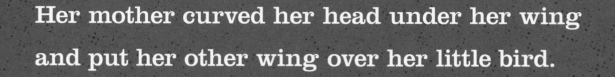
Her mother curved her head under her wing
and put her other wing over her little bird.

As the hush of the evening fell,
the crickets sang their cricket song.

And the little bird dreamed
from the warmth of the nest
of the North and the South
and the East and the West.

In the bright new light of the rising sun

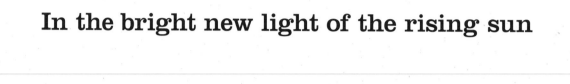

she stretched her little wings and flew.

And she flew on the wind to the North,
to a land of ice and snow,

where everything was white.

But it was too cold for the little bird
to rest or build her nest.

And so she flew around
the North Pole
and headed South.

'Til the sea was blue, and the trees were green,

and the thickets were full of flowers.

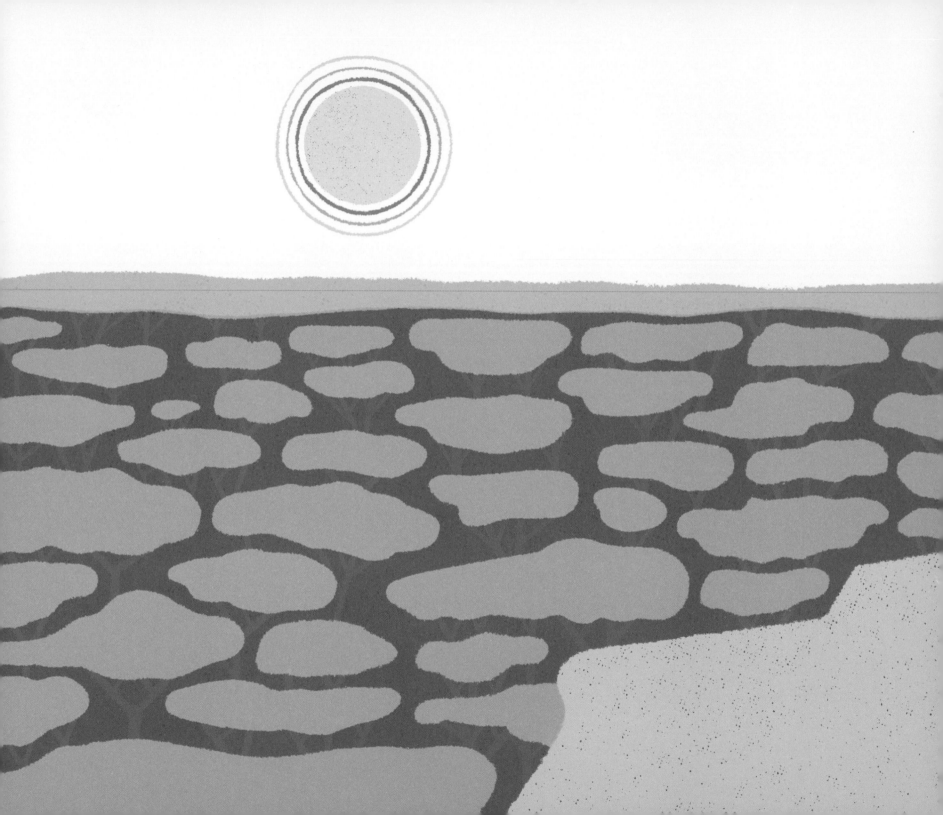

But it was too hot there to build a nest,

so the little bird rested and then she headed West.

Over mountains and rivers and plains

to where the red sun sank into the sea.

She had flown to the North
and the South and the West.
But which direction
did she like best?

She sat on a rock by the edge of the sea.

And she thought of her home in the sycamore tree.

She had flown to the North
and the South and the West.
But the East was home.

So she stretched her wings

and flew into the rising sun.

Over the high mountains,

over the deep canyons,

over the great forests

and plains

she flew.

'Til she came to where the land was soft and green with rain,

and the sycamore trees grew tall.

In the spring
when the wild birds sing
in the wild green forests
of the East

the little bird—a big bird now—

sang to her eggs

the song her mother had sung to her

'til her little birds

cracked out of their shells.

And they opened their beaks and said,
"When we fly away,
which is best,
North, South, East, or West?"